I dedicate this book to Heather, Tricia, Larissa, Jill, Tabitha, and Sandra. They are truly a blessing to my dental practice with their work ethic, dedication, care, and professionalism. I am proud to call them my co-workers and my friends.

-Dr. Gina Collins Mancini,
Family and Cosmetic Dentist

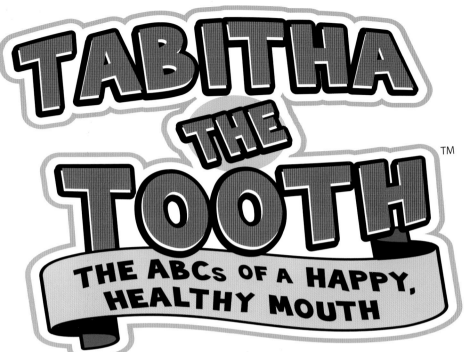

TABITHA THE TOOTH™

THE ABCs OF A HAPPY, HEALTHY MOUTH

Written by
**Dr. Gina Collins Mancini,
Family and Cosmetic Dentist**

Illustrated by
Patrick Carlson

Meet Tabitha the Tooth. She is a bright, shiny, and strong tooth. Tabitha lives in Smile City with her nineteen brothers and sisters. Tabitha stays strong and healthy by following the ABCs of a happy, healthy mouth.

A - Always try to make good food and drink choices

B - Brush AND Floss

C - Check-ups at your dentist TWICE A YEAR

Teeth are some of the strongest parts of our bodies, but we have to work at keeping them that way.

Always try to make good food and drink choices

Tabitha was hungry and had trouble deciding what snack to choose. She thought about having a piece of candy...But, she knew that candy had a lot of sugar and eating a LOT of candy would cause her to have cavities.

LOTS OF SUGAR = CAVITIES

A cavity is formed when the bacteria that live in our mouths turns the sugar that we eat into acid. This acid attacks our shiny, white tooth enamel and makes a hole in it. This hole is called a cavity.

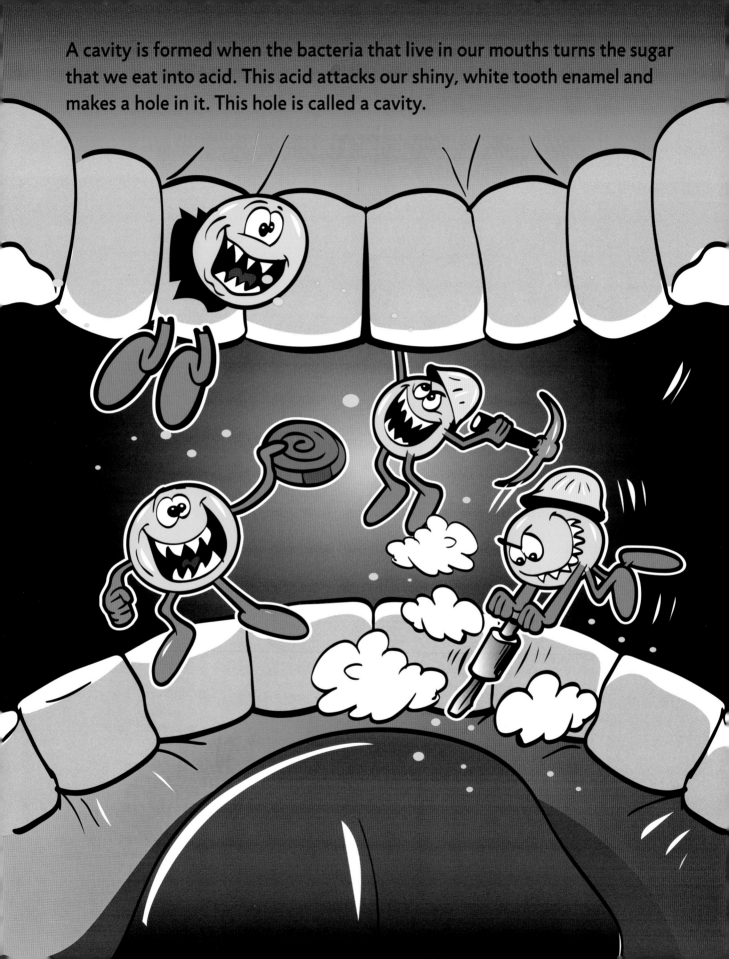

Tabitha decided she needed to try harder to make a better food choice. *What about a carrot?* she thought. Carrots are vegetables and she knew fruits and vegetables were full of good nutrients. Tabitha decided a carrot was a much better choice for her snack!

NUTRITIOUS SNACKS = HEALTHY TEETH
WAY TO GO, TABITHA!

If you have trouble remembering to make good food choices, put Tabitha the Tooth in your kitchen. She will help remind you.

Tabitha had a long day and was so tired. She was so tired that she went to bed WITHOUT brushing and flossing. When Tabitha fell asleep she had a dream...Her friends, Toby the Toothbrush and Flo the Floss, came to visit. "Tabitha," they said, "you know that in order to keep your teeth and gums healthy you need to brush TWO TIMES A DAY AND FLOSS ONCE A DAY. Wake up! Wake up!" they shouted.

Tabitha popped out of bed, marched to the bathroom, set her tooth timer for TWO MINUTES, and brushed her teeth. She remembered her favorite dentist, Doctor M, telling her that in order to remove all of the plaque germs, it is recommended that you brush for TWO minutes, TWO times a day. So she keeps a timer by the sink to help her know how long to brush. Plaque is a sticky, colorless film that forms on our teeth. Plaque can cause cavities, gum disease, and bad breath. YUCK! Tabitha did not want any plaque on her teeth. Brushing helps remove the plaque ON the teeth and flossing helps remove the plaque that is BETWEEN the teeth. After brushing and flossing, Tabitha headed back to bed.

Tabitha had a visit with Doctor M tomorrow. Doctor M would be very proud of the right choices she was making. This time when Tabitha fell asleep, she dreamed of Toby the Toothbrush and Flo the Floss dancing around a field of flowers and teddy bears. If you have trouble remembering to brush and floss, put Tabitha beside your bed. She will help remind you.

C

Check-ups at your dentist
TWICE A YEAR

Tabitha woke up just as the sun began to shine down on Smile City. She got out of bed, made a great food and drink choice for breakfast, then brushed and flossed before heading out to see Doctor M.

At Doctor M's office, Tabitha saw her friend Tanner the Tooth in the waiting room. Tabitha and Tanner talked about which flavor of fluoride they would choose. Tabitha's favorite was bubble gum and Tanner's favorite was grape. Heidi the Hygienist called for Tabitha, and she waved goodbye to Tanner.

A hygienist is a person that will clean your teeth with special toothbrushes and take pictures of your teeth with special cameras. These pictures are called radiographs. The hygienist may then put fluoride bubbles on your teeth that will help keep them strong and healthy. Heidi let Tabitha choose the flavor of the fluoride bubbles. Tabitha's favorite was bubble gum. Wow! Heidi showed Tabitha how shiny her teeth were and then went to get Doctor M.

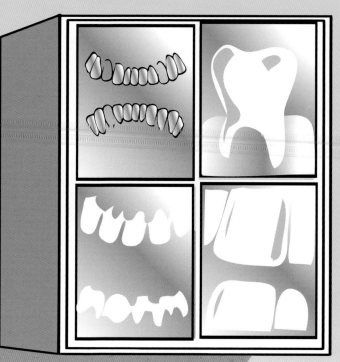

Doctor M came in and looked at her pictures. She then used her mirror and tooth counter to examine her teeth. Your dentist may also use little puffs of air to dry your teeth so that she can see just how shiny they are! Sometimes, your dentist may recommend that you use a fluoride rinse after brushing and flossing every night. This is one more thing that you can do to help keep your teeth strong and free of cavities.

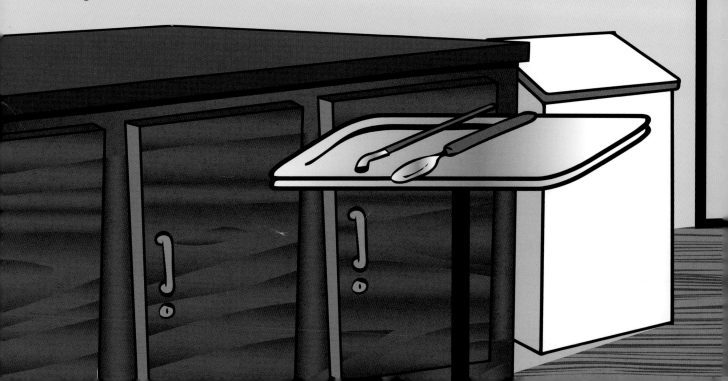

Doctor M said, "I can tell that you have been trying to make good food choices, brushing and flossing, and keeping up with your dental visits. You get an A+! Great job and keep up the good work. See you in six months!"

Tabitha said goodbye to Heidi and Doctor M. She was excited about continuing to make good choices to keep her teeth and gums healthy. She is excited about helping you too! Tabitha knows that sometimes it is not easy to make the right choice. Place Tabitha in your bedroom, bathroom, or your kitchen. She can also go with you to your dentist and watch over you as you get your check-up!

A+

I want you to make good choices about your teeth and gums!

I want you to get an A+ too!

As a full-time practicing dentist in Jacksonville, North Carolina and mother of five children, Dr. Gina Mancini knows the challenges that we face to help our children keep their teeth and gums healthy. Dr. Mancini was asked several years ago to speak at a local elementary school during dental health month. She decided that instead of taking models and poster boards into the classroom, she would write a play about Tabitha the Tooth and the choices she makes to keep her teeth and gums healthy. With the help of her amazing staff, they went on to entertain and educate many children over the next three years. In 2014, Dr. Mancini decided to turn her play into a book. With the help of this book and the Tabitha the Tooth doll, Dr. Mancini hopes to inspire your children to keep their teeth and gums healthy.

Have a book idea?

Contact us at:

Mascot Books
560 Herndon Parkway
Suite 120
Herndon, VA 20170

info@mascotbooks.com | www.mascotbooks.com